Fulfilling Katie's Needs

MIA MAE LYNNE

a "Southern Men Don't Fall in Love" short story

Published by: Book & Spirit, LLC

Cover Credit: Lex Hupertz

Edited by: Lex Hupertz

ISBN: 1-943651-11-6
ISBN-13: 978-1-943651-11-5

DEDICATION

To the almighty God of Love and Light

*"Please bless this book so all readers can enjoy in
the manner in which the angels and spirit guides
have intended."*

To my parents Johnnie Mae Parker (May 1, 1937 –
April 23, 2013) and Carl Parker (April 5, 1929 –
February 25, 2009)

*"The lessons you gave me will follow me through
eternity."*

To my sons Carlos and Marcus

*"Follow your dreams and the rewards will be
beyond anything you can ever imagine."*

To my friend Linda Smithers

*"Diamonds are a girl's best friend. Your
encouragement and guidance has helped me
overcome seemingly impossible obstacles just by
being you. You are truly my diamond."*

To my friend Melissa Montgomery.

"I admire how you handle any disastrous situation with the grace and poise of the southern belle that you are. You have a gifted ability to capture the lighter side of life and spread sunshine to those who are fortunate to get to know you."

For Noel Marion, my first complete series reader

"Thank you for believing in me and taking the time to inspire me to reach for more."

For my best friend Dolphis Sloan (June 9, 1965 – February 14, 1998)

"As my big brother, you took me under your wing in my teen years and encouraged me to follow your lead in going to the University of Akron. You are a genuinely kind free spirit and even after all these years, you are still dearly missed."

ACKNOWLEDGEMENTS

"For all others who have graciously given their time to support me through the writing process, I humbly express my thanks" – Mia Mae Lynne

Kim, Dawn, Kelli & Marcella
Earth Family

Lex Hupertz
Tiffani Keaton
Mandy Varley
Nicole Westbrook
Nicole Zavodny

My Tribe

LIGHT WORKERS

"Light workers are those who are brought to earth and are unselfishly dedicated to giving their time to shine their light on humanity and make the world a better place." – Mia Mae Lynne

Debi J. Fellows
Spirals of Spirit, Painesville, Ohio

Effie Kapodistrias
Effie's Divine Celebration, Oakville, ON

Nicole Westbrook
Inner Fyre, Mentor, Ohio

Chapter 1

What a wonderful day to be Katie Pennington Leigh.

After a long week training corporate executives on the importance of International Traffic in Arms Regulations (ITAR), Katie had been asked by her CEO to be the leader in educating her coworkers globally on the same practices. Her career was skyrocketing! And she was finally getting the chance to head home to Atlanta, only a nine-hour flight in the way of her house and her husband.

She smiled to herself. Her slide presentation had gone wonderfully. It had gotten her the promotion, and even if it meant a bit more travelling, the pay raise and the prestige...excellent.

Great job. Great home. And a great husband.

Katie smiled and jerked when the stewardess tapped her on the shoulder to tell her to put her seatback up for takeoff.

She'd spent months preparing for the seminar and it had now put her in the spotlight to becoming the subject matter expert in Export Compliance. She trained a hundred employees of her aerospace company and her fluency in Spanish and French allowed her to answer questions without missing a beat.

The stewardess asked if she'd like anything to drink before takeoff and Katie asked the stewardess for a cup of coffee.

The privileges of a well-deserved upgrade to First Class.

Katie pulled out a few of her notes to review, sipping on her coffee, before settling in for a much-needed rest and dreams of her husband's reaction when she told him the good news that night.

She was arriving a day earlier than expected. She could get her nails done like she hadn't been able to while in Paris. As Director of Export Controls, she needed to maintain a polished image. And she needed a bit of downtime after all her hard work. Just a manicure. Nothing excessive.

She'd schedule a time to meet Mario at the studio for a personal workout. She hadn't had a chance to work out with him before leaving, what with all her preparations and so forth. It would be good to get her personal trainer back in for a session.

A workout. Kale smoothie refresher. Then an afternoon of planning for when her husband got home from work that night.

Katie wasn't the type to blush on an airplane, but thinking about her husband brought color to her cheeks.

Her hotel tycoon was handsome and sexy and the slight age difference between them only heightened her attraction to him. Richard Leigh was everything she wanted in a man: well-polished, athletic, and with an appreciation for the fine arts.

Katie had lucked out in her second marriage.

She couldn't wait to surprise him with her early return from the seminar. She had so much to tell him about the people and connections she'd made.

***

She peered out the window at the bright sunny sky in Atlanta as the plane landed at noon. It was refreshing to be home and away from the gray and rainy London she'd left behind.

She strolled through the airport with heels clicking over the tiles on her way to baggage claim. She collected her things and headed towards long-term parking and her car.

Katie pulled up to her driveway, and recognized her best friend, Andrea's, silver Porsche blocking the garage.

"What's she doing here?"

Katie left her suitcase in the car as she entered her town home and called out for Richard.

There was no reply, though his car had been in the garage on her way in.

Carefully, Katie made her way up the stairs. There was a rhythmic pounding against the wall coming from the master bedroom. She could hear panting and moaning the closer she got.

The sounds were louder, and she could hear distinct voices as she peered through the opening in the doorway.

"Oh Richard! Baby! Do it to me; don't stop!"

"Fuck yes."

Katie pushed the bedroom door open further. She could see Richard's ass pounding into the spread legs wrapped around his waist. She might not have been able to see Andrea's face, but she knew the woman's voice well enough.

She watched as the pair climaxed, her husband calling out her friend's name while the bitch stroked his back and cooed at him.

"I love —"

Katie stepped away from the door, not wanting to hear anything else. She pulled it gently closed with her, trying to hide herself from the couple in the room.

How could Andrea do this to her?

How could Richard?

Wasn't she enough for her husband?

She'd thought they were happy, goddamnit!

The bed squeaked and Katie heard the giggling Barbie laugh of her ex-friend approaching the door.

Before Katie could run, Andrea pulled it open and Katie straightened her back to meet the woman's gaze.

Andrea screamed and Richard came running.

Richard sucked in a shocked breath when he saw Katie. His mouth opened and closed and Katie watched as he shook his head and swallowed once before managing to speak. "I thought you were out of town."

He thought I was out of town. "You thought I was out of town?" Katie clenched her hands into fists, fought not to punch her lying, cheating, bastard of a husband in the nose. "You thought I was out of town." Like that was any excuse?

"Katie...Richard and I, we uh..." Andrea stammered.

"Save it, bitch." She turned her glare between the two naked people in front of her. "Get the hell out of my house."

"Katie, let's talk—"

"Get the fuck out of here, Richard!" She closed her eyes, the image of the two of them having sex burned into her brain. "Get out of my house!"

Chapter 2

Katie tried to pull herself together.

An important person like her didn't have the luxury of falling apart.

Her life was perfect. Her life had to be perfect. She'd organized every step of her life to make it that way.

Her career was carefully compartmentalized into deadlines and meetings. Each evening had some event that she and Richard were supposed to go to together. She even made sure she had time to go to the opera with him and rescheduled her Pilates around that.

She was doing everything in her power to be a good wife to him.

Katie swiped angrily at the tears on her face.

"Fucking asshole."

She'd left her briefcase in the kitchen when she entered the house. That was probably a safe place to go. No hint of Richard in there since he never cooked anyways. She wouldn't be reminded of him there. She could think about work and her planner.

Surely there was something in her planner that she could focus on other than her life falling apart.

The page was blank.

"No."

She wasn't supposed to be back in town yet. She hadn't registered for the seminar at her office because she was supposed to still be in London and hadn't moved things around in her schedule because she and Richard…

Fuck.

"There's got to be something to do. My life is not a blank page."

It was barely three in the afternoon.

Everything had changed at noon and it was only now three o'clock.

The end of her life as she knew it was taking forever and she didn't know what to do.

She could go back to the office before rush hour traffic got bad. Maybe she could find a salon that would take her for a manicure but what was the point? No one was going to see.

She picked up her purse and her planner and opened the door to the garage.

Richard was standing there.

"What do you want!" She screamed at him.

"I want to talk to you."

"I have nothing to say to you!" She shouted.

He entered the house, keeping himself between the door and her exit. He snarled, "That's the problem. You don't have time for me."

"Bullshit Richard! I always make time for you. I just got back from traveling and you were the first person I wanted to see. My career—"

"That's just it, Katie. Your career comes before everything including your husband. We've been married two years and other than our honeymoon we've never spent any time together. I kept waiting for you to slow down and every time I would make plans to get away for a week with us alone, you found an excuse not to go. Your compromise was a long weekend with your Goddamn planner and a briefcase full of work!

"You called the office five times on our honeymoon trip to Hawaii. Stepped away from dinner nearly every night to take calls. We've never had a conversation that lasted longer than ten minutes because you are preoccupied with your *career*."

He practically sneered the word at her and Katie jerked back like it was a physical assault.

She stepped away, shaking her head, wanting to run.

Richard grabbed her arm. "Stay here and talk to me. I deserve that."

Katie pulled her arm away, held her briefcase to her chest like it could protect her. "You knew that I had a big career and lots of responsibilities when you met me. I thought we understood each other. This is who I am."

"I see that quite clearly." He shook his head, sneered as he looked her over. "Why the hell did you agree to marry me if you had no time for me?"

"Don't make this my fault you lying, cheating bastard. Why didn't you come to Europe with me instead of fucking one of my friends?"

Richard snorted in disgust. "Yeah, let's go to Europe so you can ignore me on another continent? I want time with my wife. I don't want to be your personal stand up man because you need to show up to an event with a date."

"Yet you're the one having an affair. You don't want time with me. Go back to fucking Andrea."

Richard shook his head and met Katie's gaze. "At least she has time for me."

He didn't wait for her response, leaving through the door he'd blocked her escape from.

She stood there in shock, trying to tell herself this wasn't her fault.

The little voice in the back of her mind kept whispering that maybe it was.

Chapter 3

Katie spent the next few days dedicating herself to her work. She spent late hours at the office and pampered herself with manicures, pedicures and new clothes.

Retail therapy.

Nothing like a new Gucci bag to try and put a smile on her face.

She managed to rearrange her hair appointment for Thursday evening after work. The stylist wrapped her in curlers and put her under the dryer while the woman took care of another customer.

What was she to do now? She didn't have time to go through another divorce. That was not in her plan. Who was she going to call? Her attorney for her last divorce was so incompetent that she had to draw up her own divorce papers and buffer the demands. There had to be someone that she could trust but…

"Doug!" She said out loud.

Embarrassed by her outburst, she looked around to see if anyone had noticed.

She sank lower in her seat but finally managed to relax.

Katie would give Doug a call. He was an attorney in Atlanta. He'd know who to call if he didn't do divorces. And he'd been so nice that one date they'd had. Why hadn't she ever followed up with that?

He'd be able to help her though, she was sure.

Katie closed her eyes and felt the first real smile to cross her lips since everything blew up.

Chapter 4

Katie entered Doug's high rise office building at the King and Queen Towers in Downtown Atlanta at noon on Friday. She waited about fifteen minutes before the receptionist led her back to his office.

Doug looked up as she entered the door. He was still as handsome as ever: tall, tanned, sandy blond hair and deep blue eyes.

And when he smiled, damn, those eyes lit up.

Nothing like eye candy to make your troubles melt away.

"Come in Mrs. Leigh and have a seat." Doug rose to assist her with her chair. He'd always had impeccable southern manners.

"Please, it's Katie. It won't be Leigh much longer."

Doug returned to his desk, clicked his pen, and pulled out a blank yellow legal pad. He sat upright met her gaze with an understanding smile. "It's good to see you but not under these circumstances. I got the message that you wanted a divorce and had my secretary schedule you in. Can you tell me a little of what's going on?"

Katie took a deep breath. No tears. No weakness. She was in control of her life, not Richard, not anyone else. This was just another calendar filled day with a teeny little visit to a divorce attorney.

Nothing devastating.

This marriage was not that important.

It was time to move on.

Katie burst into tears.

The pep talk didn't help.

"That lying cheating bastard was sleeping with my best friend!"

Doug was still for a moment, and then moved to get a box of tissues and offer them to her. "I'm so sorry."

Katie swiped a few and dabbed at her eyes, embarrassed by her outburst. "It's ok, please don't apologize. I don't know where that came from."

"I'd say probably from your lying, cheating bastard husband."

Katie managed a small hiccupped laugh at Doug's attempted joke. "Thank you. You probably hear this all the time."

"Each case is different, but you're not alone. You don't have to go through this alone. Just take your time. Tell me what happened and what you would like for me to do."

Katie talked about how Richard and she had met, about the way he proposed and how great the wedding was, how hard the last two years had been with work and trying to build a relationship between them but she'd thought it was working. She'd thought that she and Richard were perfect up until she walked in the house and found him with Andrea.

She told Doug everything just…broke.

"I'm so sorry, Katie." He looked down at the notepad and then met her gaze,

"Will you take my case?"

"Let me confer with my partners. I think a friend of mine would be better suited to your case. I want to make sure that Richard pays for his indiscretion and make sure that you have the best attorney with a clear conscious representing you without bias of any kind."

"What!" Katie exclaimed in between sniffles. "What are you saying? You don't want my case? But I know you. I trust *you* to handle this."

Doug rose from his desk, walked over and brushed his hand lightly on her shoulder. Katie looked up with her eyes still full of tears.

Doug returned her gaze. "It's not good to mix business with pleasure. I would like to have the pleasure of seeing you after this business is over."

Oh.

Doug smiled warmly.

Katie blushed, took a deep breath and smiled back at him.

Very smooth, she thought to herself.

Doug brushed a stray strand of hair back from her forehead behind her ear. "Let me go check with Harold and I'll be right back."

He left the door partially closed and she sat in her chair, hands restless as she waited for him to return.

Doug walked back in with a handsome man at his shoulder, both good looking specimens that made her heart beat a bit faster, especially when her blond god met her gaze. "I want to introduce you to my associate, Mr. Harold Morgan."

Harold extended his hand and Katie started to rise.

"No, please stay seated." Harold took the chair next to her and Doug returned to his desk.

"Doug briefly told me about your case and, Mrs. Leigh, I'm so sorry that a genteel woman such as yourself should have borne witness to such an immoral act. Our firm is ready to stand with you and make that miscreant pay for his misdeeds."

Katie smiled at his words. Between these two men, that bastard was going to pay for this. "So I can count on you to represent me?"

Harold reached in his pocket and handed her his card. "Of course you can count on me to represent you. Amy is my personal secretary and she will find a time for us to meet to further discuss your situation."

"Thank you so much." Katie said as she shook his hand when he stood to leave.

Harold walked to the door and looked back at Doug.

Doug nodded back and Harold walked out the door pulling the knob behind him.

"You'll like Harold. He's a good attorney, and I'll assist with the case where needed but I won't be directly involved in the case."

"He seems like a nice man."

"He is, but he's a dog in the courtroom." Doug met her gaze, let his eyes roam over her in more than attorney-client privilege.

His smile turned wicked and Katie enjoyed the burst of pride at his gaze

"I'm sure you have a lot to take care of," he stood, walking towards her, "so I'll walk you out."

She let him take her hand and help her up. "You don't have to. I'll be fine." She smiled and squeezed his hand, let her gaze roam like his, acknowledging the unspoken desires between them. "Thank you so much, Doug. We should catch up sometime, like you said, after my divorce."

He nodded and she turned to leave his office. "Anytime, you have my number."

"I certainly do."

Chapter 5

Katie took Doug's advice and hired Harold to represent her in her divorce. The proceedings were like her first separation. Despite Richard's protests, the case was settled with relatively few disagreements. She got the house, and he claimed their boat. Once the decree was signed and the attorneys shook hands, Katie walked out the door glad to be rid of her ex and looking forward to brighter prospects in the future.

Richard stopped her as she was walking out of the law office.

"Sorry it didn't work," he said solemnly.

"It would have worked if you didn't cheat."

"Well you lied."

"What are you talking about?"

"Andrea said that you can't have children."

Katie gasped at his unexpected statement. "Andrea is not a doctor. You never asked me about children."

Richard looked at her, his face turning bright red. "Well if I wanted children, you couldn't have had any."

Katie's mind quickly flashed to her irregular cycle and the many pregnancy tests she took only to find out that they were negative. She'd never told Richard any of that. She wanted motherhood to be a special surprise for him. She'd never gotten pregnant with her first ex-husband Dave. She'd never been tested to see if she was the problem, never taken any tests or gone to any clinics, but Richard had never asked her about any of that either.

It could have just been the wrong time, for all she knew, but he jumped to conclusions, right alongside Andrea.

She straightened her shoulders and met his stare. "I never said that! And even if I had, Richard, we could always have adopted." She shook her head, done with him for good now. "This conversation is over and the marriage is dissolved. Have this discussion with Andrea."

"Andrea is expecting."

Katie's face turned white.

Her ex-best friend was pregnant with her ex-husband's baby.

Wasn't that just the icing on the cake?

"I hope it's yours. God knows who else that whore has been sleeping with..." She couldn't help the hurt smile, victorious at having made him cringe, that crossed her lips. "Oh, sorry, I guess you thought that you were her only sperm donor in town."

Katie turned and walked away, quickly pushing the buttons on the elevator to escape him.

Richard moved as though to follow her, and Katie abandoned the elevator for the stairs, taking the fifteen floors by foot rather than riding in a small car with that bastard.

Besides, she needed some time to think and air to breathe.

She found her car and managed to get in the driver's seat before her tears started. The flood lasted for fifteen minutes until her face was splotchy and her eyes burned, but it was over.

It was over.

She was single again.

She gave Doug a call.

"You've got Bader"

Katie managed to sniffle though her response. "Doug? It's Katie. From college? We spoke a few months ago regarding my divorce?"

She heard papers shuffle on the other end of the line before he answered.

"Of course. How are you? You sound upset, Katie."

"The divorce was final today."

"I'm sorry, Katie."

She sniffled again. "Thank you. I was wondering if you were free to meet up, like we said in your office."

He was silent and she wondered what he was thinking about, knew he was a player, remembered it from his smile. Nothing serious. A fling with Doug would be safe. Nothing serious. Katie squeezed the phone tightly as she awaited his response.

"I can't tonight. What about Friday instead? I think you need to get over the shock first and then we can get together."

"Sure. Of course. Actually, that's better for me too. I'll check my calendar and call you to confirm?"

"Sounds like a plan."

"Great," Katie hoped he couldn't hear the false excitement in her voice. He was right. She was in no shape to be on a date tonight anyways. "I'll talk to you soon then."

"Sure."

He disconnected first and Katie sat in her car staring at the black box in her hand.

All the convenience of technology yet all alone and no one to talk to.

Katie dried the remaining tears and looked in the mirror.

"I look awful." Her eyes were swollen and cheeks splotchy from her tears. She'd need a facial to get the puffiness out of her face.

Katie pulled out her planner and searched for her next open hour or two where she could schedule something.

She had a French club meeting at 7:00 p.m. but was free from now till then. That gave her a few hours to kill but, she looked back at her face in the mirror.

She didn't want to have to explain her whole story to an uncaring technician.

Besides, she did have one person she could always count on to have her back. Just because she'd asked her dad not to come today, didn't mean she didn't rely on his support.

And if she left now, she'd have just enough time to get to the country club and talk to him before she had to head back to the office.

Chapter 6

Katie sat in the car for a few moments freshening up her makeup. She wanted her dad to see that she was brave and facing her challenges head on. Her dad was paying for the divorce, he'd never liked Richard anyway, and he didn't ask her a lot of questions. She appreciated her dad not giving her a hard time.

Her shoes clicked noisily on the cream-colored marble tile as she walked through Dupree Country Club making her way to the back of the building where the bar overlooked the plush green golf course and southern style brick mansions. Her dad sat chuckling away in conversation with the bartender and a young woman enthralled with his every word.

She slowed her pace and walked over to him, tapping him on the shoulder to be recognized.

He turned to her with a warm smile, pulling her into his arms for a long hug. "How's my ferocious tiger? Did you take Richard to the cleaners?"

Katie smiled. Her dad knew how to boost her ego. Stay strong. There were too many people watching and reputation is everything. "I certainly got what I wanted and I expected nothing less."

"That's my girl. Have a seat." He turned away to speak to the woman next to him. "Susan, this is my daughter, Katie; Katie, Susan."

Susan's dark eyes sparkled as she waved a hello. Katie continued to smile and nod back. Her dad was a man who kept a lot of female company in and out of his bed. Katie passed this woman off as another temporary fling.

"She's a director at Parker Logistics specializing in Export Compliance." Don turned back to Katie, smiling at his date. "Susan's husband owns the Blakely Porsche dealership."

"Impressive," was all that Katie could find to say. She must have heard him wrong, but then, her dad didn't care about relationships. His had never worked out either. Why would he care about this woman whose marriage he could potentially ruin too? "I don't mean to be rude, Susan, but I really need to speak to my dad privately."

Susan smiled at Katie and looked at Don. "Your daughter needs you. I'll come back later. Nice to meet you Katie." Susan slid off her barstool and almost twisted her ankle as she stepped on her three-inch heel sideways. Don moved to catch her fall.

"Are you all right?"

"Yes, I'm fine." As soon as she caught her balance, she limped slightly away to give Katie and Don some space.

"What's going on? What really happened in court?"

"Let's go find a table. I don't want to talk to you at the bar and I don't want your girlfriend hearing about my divorce." Katie let out an exasperated huff. The last thing she wanted now was to deal with her dad and his indiscretions.

"Susan's just a friend, Kaitlin. Show some respect." Don waved to the bartender to bring his tab.

"Sure. I know you, Dad. You're a player. I just can't believe you'd think this was okay after everything I've just been through.

"Katie!"

"I can't believe, after everything I'm going through, you're sleeping with someone else's wife."

Susan returned and Katie continued her outburst. "Susan, how can you think that this is right to treat your spouse this way? It's because of people like you so many hard-working couples end up in divorce. I thought you were better than this, Dad."

"That is enough." Don stood from his barstool and glared at his daughter. "I taught you better than that."

She snorted. "Way to lead by example, Dad." She turned her gaze to Susan, didn't try to hide her sneer. "Ms. Susan, please accept my apologies for my outburst. I just don't have any tolerance for lying and cheating behavior today." Katie turned on her heels and stormed out of the bar.

Don quickly rose and spoke to Susan. "My daughter's divorce has been difficult. I apologize for her behavior. I'll return later."

Don quickly caught up with Katie as she was headed to the parking lot. As soon as he was outside, he let out a shout. "KATIE"

Katie froze in her tracks still fuming from what she saw. The man that she needed to talk to was busy with his own indiscretions!

He walked closer to her. "We need to talk. Now!"

Katie approached her dad. She was close enough to see the disappointment in his eyes. "I can't handle this right now."

"Let's go inside and discuss this."

Katie marched back into the Dupree Country club with her left fist clenched gritting her teeth as she approached her dad. They walked together to find a hostess.

"I need a private table. Will you take us to one?"

"Certainly."

Katie was first behind the hostess careful not to knock into the tables along the way. She yanked the chair from the table not waiting for her dad to pull the seat for her and plopped herself down, putting her elbows on the table and her full face in her hands.

The hostess quickly removed herself which left Don to carefully take a seat across from Katie. He opened the conversation with a patient sigh, carefully choosing his words. "This has been a tough day for you. I'm glad it's over."

Katie carefully fought back the inkling of tears that were starting to form in the corners of her eyelids. She was with her dad and he wasn't going to see her break down. She lifted her head and formed a weak smile. "Yes, it has."

Don took his napkin and placed it on his lap. He looked around and summoned a waiter to come to the table. The waiter acknowledged his motions and was there momentarily at the table.

"May I help you, sir?"

"I'll have a bottle of Dom please. My daughter and I are celebrating."

"Celebrating? Celebrating what?" She frowned at her father, the tears she was fighting about to win the battle against her will. "I just got divorced."

"And that is why we're celebrating." Don nodded and waived the waiter away to bring his order.

"You're calling this a celebration. That asshole just told me that Andrea is pregnant. Are we going to celebrate that too?"

Don's face turned grim. "Just be glad you aren't carrying his baby. This divorce would have been more of a nightmare."

Katie let out a loud sigh and sat back in her chair. Her dad was right. What if they both were pregnant? She would be stuck as a single mother.

She had a career to think of. She wasn't ready to be a parent.

She took a deep breath for strength.

That prick actually did her a favor.

The waiter returned to the table and poured the champagne.

Don raised his glass and Katie raised hers. "Here's to new beginnings." He tilted his glass to hers making a soft clink before taking his sip.

Katie took a big swallow.

"Are you ok?"

"Yes. I need a new beginning more than you know."

"I've got to run to my meeting."

"You just got here. Why are you rushing off so soon? I want to hear more about the proceedings today."

"Dad, you have company to keep you busy. I've got my meetings. I only had a short time between court and my next one to see you." She tried a smile that her dad met without matching the expression. "Let me check my planner and we'll have lunch this week."

"Call my secretary and check with her so we don't have a conflict. You've rescheduled three times in the last two weeks. I want time with my daughter."

"I'm sorry, Dad" She got up from her chair and hugged him as she whispered in his ear, "This divorce has been tough and the job demanding. I'll make time for us. I promise."

Chapter 7

Katie cleared off her Friday calendar so she could prepare for her date with Doug. She called her friend Melinda to see if she was free to go shopping and was waiting for the woman at the door to her house when Melinda arrived in her black Bentley Turbo.

Instead of inviting Melinda in, she grabbed her purse and planner and sat in the passenger side of the car. Melinda was wearing dark shades and her fingernails were a glossy red that clicked against the steering wheel when she tapped on it. Her Louis Vuitton purse was open on the seat exhibiting all her belongings including a wad of cash. Katie tried to warn Melinda to keep her purse closed but Melinda lived in her own fantasy world of everyone being rich and catering to her needs.

"Lenox or Phipps?" Melinda asked with a bright smile. "Lenox has Nieman Marcus and Phipps has Saks. If we have time, we can go to both stores."

"Definitely Lenox first."

Katie settled in her seat as Melinda pulled out of the driveway. She opened her planner to see how much time she'd allotted for shopping.

Melinda looked over and sighed with disgust. "Will you put that away and let's talk about the divorce. You didn't have time to give me the details. What happened?"

"Richard and I finalized everything last week and Andrea is pregnant."

"WHAT!" Melinda slammed on the brakes and looked around to make sure she wasn't going to get rear-ended for stopping so suddenly. She pulled over and parked the car on the side of the road. With a quick flick, she'd freed her seatbelt and turned so that she was facing Katie who was staring resolutely out the window in front of her. "When did you find this out?"

Katie took a breath and relaxed her death grip on the door handle, slowly relaxing once the car had settled and she could pick up her planner which laid scattered on the floor in front of her. Exasperated, she said, "It will take me thirty minutes to put this back together. I don't have time for this, Mel."

"Never mind the planner." She reached over and put her hands over Katie's in Katie's lap. "Tell me about Andrea and her being pregnant. Is it Richards? Is he sure? How rich would it be if she was cheating on him, the bastard? Andrea has a lot of boyfriends."

"I don't know. I don't want to know. He says it is, but I don't really know." She met her friend's gaze, the ever-hungry gossip lapping up every word

Katie spoke. "Do we have to talk about this now? I want to get ready for my date with Doug."

"Yes we have to talk about this now. You are refusing to let it bother you. Doesn't this bother you at all that one of your ex-best friends is pregnant with your ex-husband's baby? Aren't you upset? The only thing you are worried about is that planner. What did your therapist say?"

Melinda tended to wear her emotions on her sleeve and had little respect for anyone who didn't act the same way.

That didn't mean Katie was going to kowtow to her. And Melinda didn't need to know everything about Katie's life. "I don't have time for therapy. Maybe I can schedule that in next month." Katie tried for flippant even as she fought back the tears that were forming in her eyes. She pulled dark shades from her purse and put them on so Melinda wouldn't notice.

Melinda returned her gaze to the windshield, tapping away at her steering wheel again. "Therapy's not a bad thing, Katie. This has got to be tough for you. I don't want you to have a nervous breakdown. This is the second time that you found a woman in bed with your cheating husband. That takes a lot to recover from."

"Okay. I'll try to schedule some time with Dr. Zwinger." She tried a laugh as Melinda pulled back out into traffic. "I'm sure he will recommend that I take a vacation. That seems to be all that he recommends for me. In my last visit two years ago, he said that I should schedule more time with my husband. I didn't take his advice and now I'm divorced, again."

Melinda signaled to switch lanes and proceeded back on her route to the mall. "You should listen to him. Now that you're rid of Richard, let's spend some time out of the country. You and I could go to Italy."

Katie swallowed, focused on Melinda's statement and responded. "I can't. I have a career. I've taken too much time off with this divorce as it is. Maybe we can spend a weekend at a day spa or at the beach. I want to work on my tan."

Melinda's face brightened up. "Daddy has a friend that owns property in Destin, Florida. He can fly us there on his private plane." She was so excited about the prospect that she jerked the wheel and Katie grabbed for the handle again. "Let's do that this weekend."

So long as you're not driving or flying the plane. "I can't this weekend. I'm seeing Doug tonight remember."

"Oh, that's right. Minor detail. I thought we could leave in the morning but if he spends the night, you won't want to get up that early."

Katie smiled at her statement. She hadn't had sex in a while and couldn't remember when the last time she was with Richard prior to the divorce.

Maybe a good evening filled with sex wasn't such a bad idea.

"Let me check my calendar and plan for next weekend."

"Unless Doug wants to stick around for longer. A man in the wings and a vacation in the future. I like your style, Katie."

***

"Call me after. I want to hear all of the details."

Katie laughed as she grabbed her bags out of Melinda's crowded trunk and waved goodbye. "I will."

"You've got to look your best tonight. He could be husband number three!"

Chapter 8

Douglas Arthur Bader.

She breathed his name as she was dressing for dinner. She'd swept her hair up in a bun; she had on designer heels, a shimmering navy dress, with pearl earrings. It was a long time since she went out on a social occasion with a man that was interested in her.

It had always felt like work with Richard.

She was on her phone with her office when the doorbell rang.

Her heart raced as she made her goodbyes and promised to have an answer for a pending issue by Monday morning.

With a deep breath, she hung up her phone, touched up her lipstick in the hallway mirror, and stepped to the door to receive her guest.

He smiled at her and for a moment she couldn't look away, not even when his smile turned to a grin and she felt heat rise in her cheeks.

Doug handed her a dozen red roses.

Katie accepted the gift and lifted them to her nose to smell.

"I thought these would cheer you up," he said.

"They're perfect. Thank you."

Doug leaned toward Katie and kissed her on the cheek.

Katie blushed at his caress.

"Are you ready to go?" he asked.

"Yes."

He held out his arm and helped her out the front door, waited as she locked it behind her and followed him to his car. Doug opened the door of his cobalt blue Mercedes and assisted Katie into his ride.

They went to an Italian restaurant where Doug had reserved a table for them. He ordered a bottle of the Greco di Tufo, an imported Italian wine from the south.

Katie smiled at his choice.

Richard was a wine connoisseur. She'd learned a lot from her ex-husband, enough to know that Doug's choice was impeccable.

The waiter handed her the cork along with a small taste of the wine. After swirling it to look at the color and sniffing for the smell of the grapes, she took a small sip. Doug patiently watched as Katie demonstrated her expertise.

"Is it to your liking?" the waiter asked.

Doug was also watching for her approval.

"Splendid."

The waiter smiled and poured her a fresh glass before doing the same for Doug.

"Did we come here when we went out a few years ago?" Katie asked.

"We did," Doug replied. "I'm surprised you remember." He leaned back in his seat. "I think that was the shortest date I ever had."

"It was?" Katie said with her eyebrows crinkled in confusion. "How so?"

"You were working late at the office and agreed to meet me here. We ordered the same bottle of wine. After it was poured, you disappeared for ten minutes, came back and told me you had an emergency to settle at the office and promised me another date. Your calendar was full every time I called you. I was surprised to learn through mutual friends that you got married. I don't know where you found the time."

Katie laughed, "Dicky was very persistent. I had to create time in my calendar. He was at a lot of restaurants that I frequented. We started having dinner together and it developed from there." Katie inhaled with the memories. "I guess that's over now."

The thought of that bastard having a baby with her ex-best friend wasn't as unemotional as she'd implied to Melinda. She blinked her eyes and focused on the eye candy in front of her. She tried a weak smile.

Doug got the hint that talking about the divorce was still a painful subject. He reached into his suit jacket and handed Katie an envelope. "I got you a little surprise."

Startled, she opened it and squealed with delight. "Box seats to The Goodbye Girl! Doug! I love the musicals. Thank you. How'd you know?"

"I saw the reviews and thought you would enjoy it."

The waiter returned.

Katie requested a salad with a light vinaigrette, and Doug asked for the grilled grouper and vegetables. Her phone rang as the waiter walked away.

"You're not going to leave me again, are you?" Doug asked with a teasing wink.

"Only for a minute." She said, smiling as she stood and answered the phone. "Sandy, calm down. What did you do with the paperwork? You made a copy, didn't you?"

***

Twenty minutes later Katie was still on the phone with her office. She felt someone tap her on the shoulder and turned to see Doug standing behind her, his arms crossed and the smile forced on his perfect lips.

"The food's here and my grouper is getting cold."

Katie nodded with a whispered "I'm sorry" to Doug as she held up a finger requesting just one more minute. "I have to go, Sandy, I have a very handsome dinner date that has been very patiently waiting for me and I would love to wrap this up tomorrow. I'm out of touch by phone for the rest of the evening. Night."

Doug's cheeks tightened as he led her back to the table, solicitous as always, though, she couldn't help but notice the stiffness that seemed to envelope him now.

"I'm so sorry, Doug. I'll make it up to you, I promise. I did mean what I said. My phone is off for the evening."

"You're addicted to your career."

"Yes, I am. And it's addicted to me. Amazing how many people need me."

"Do you have a staff?"

"I have three import and export administrators and one export compliance manager. I requested in my budget to hire another export compliance manager. I've been granted my request but I just learned that my export manager has resigned and he will be leaving in two weeks. I haven't had time to do the interviews to fill both positions."

Doug nodded and reached across the table to hold Katie's hand, give it a gentle squeeze.

Katie breathed a small sigh of relief as she met his gaze and saw the understanding there. He was at least as career oriented as she was. That boded well for the night and whatever relationship they could manage together. "Thank you for understanding."

Chapter 9

It was the longest musical in the history of musicals.

Katie was not able to focus on any of the singing. She was agonizing over all the work she had to do in the office Monday morning. She'd turned off her phone and left her planner at home. She felt naked without the constant pressure of work egging her on.

But...

No, she was here to enjoy herself without interruptions from the office.

Katie sucked in a breath. She noticed the very pregnant woman next to her get up and excuse herself.

Pregnant.

Damn.

She'd never know the pleasure of having a baby. Not that she wanted one, necessarily, not now at least, but Richard and Andrea were pregnant and it should have, could have, been her, or not, but still, and she couldn't even talk to her best friend because she was now the enemy and...

She felt a light squeeze of her hand

"Are you enjoying the musical?"

She gave a faint smile as she met Doug's gaze. "Yes."

"Are you sure? You don't look happy."

Katie leaned closer to Doug and said, "It's a little slow for me. I can think of other things I'd rather do. Can we just go back to my place?"

Katie couldn't believe her boldness. She hadn't been with anyone during the separation and divorce proceedings. Hell, she hadn't been with Richard, not really, for a while before his affair either.

She wasn't divorced long but she needed to release some tension.

She was a free woman and there was no reason not to see Doug.

"Certainly."

Doug rose and Katie stood with him, a smile on her lips as she followed him from the theater.

When they arrived at her townhome thirty minutes later, Katie unpinned her hair and shook it out to its full length. Doug stood by the door waiting for her to motion for him to join her.

Her shimmering navy dress fell to the floor. Katie wore a matching navy bra and panties. She stepped over the pile to Doug, still wearing her navy high heeled shoes.

She tried a coy smile, wrapped his silk tie around her fingers to pull him with her to her bedroom. "Follow me."

Doug smiled and closed the door behind him.

Chapter 10

"Ooooh" Katie purred, rolling to the side of her bed and stretching out against the cool sheets that were warm the night before. She slid her hand up and down the sheets next to her.

Doug.

Damn, she'd needed that. She would have preferred that he'd remained for the next morning too but…

She'd asked him last night.

"You're leaving so soon?"

"I never stay. No commitments."

Katie sighed. "Right. How could I forget?" She tried to keep the agitation from her voice. "I'll get my robe and show you the way out."

Katie supposed it was a good thing Doug was gone. It would have been too much otherwise. Too much attachment. Now she could get up, take her time, not worry about entertaining another round with her horny attorney.

She didn't dare call Doug. She knew his rules. Everything was under Doug's timing and control.

One long hot shower to start the day washing away the delightful play of the night before. She must have been in for a good twenty minutes because the steam created a nice warm fog. She let out a sigh as she stepped out of the shower dabbing the towel delicately over her body not to miss a spot. Her thoughts were interrupted by her phone ringing.

"They'll call back," she said.

The phone started ringing again.

"I'll bet that's Mel. She doesn't give up." Wrapped in her towel, she moved to her dresser and picked up the phone.

"Well, how was it?" the unmistakable voice of Melinda cheerily asked. "Was it better than the ex?"

Chuckling, Katie answered, "Of course it was."

"Well, when do you see him again Miss Hot Stuff?"

"I don't know. I'm sure he'll call. I'm unforgettable."

Melinda laughed "How many times did you orgasm?"

"Three but who's counting. Mel, let me call you later. I don't want to be late to session."

***

Katie arrived late anyways. She had to cut the conversation short with Melinda because she knew that Melinda would want all the details. Melinda was a great friend but sometimes was a little bit too cheerful in the face of disastrous events. Her idea of dealing with stress was a plane ticket out of any country causing her problems.

Mario was lifting free-weights when she walked in the training room.

"Are you ready for your session today?" Mario asked in a sweet southern twang with a feminine flavor that was unmistakably Mario's trademark voice.

"Ready and willing," Katie said cheerily.

Mario and Katie trained for forty-five minutes, a round of kick boxing and then a cool down with yoga.

"And so I kicked Andrea and Richard from the house and found an attorney the next day."

"Oh honey," Mario adjusted her position for the Sarvangasana and Katie relaxed into the pose, her back legs straight in the air with her weight resting on her neck and shoulders, hand supporting her hips in the almost headstand. "I'm so sorry about the divorce. That skank was not your best friend."

Katie snorted, but it couldn't quite cover her disappointment. "Andrea's pregnant."

Mario's gaze snapped to hers. "Oh no she didn't. That ho did not get pregnant! Oh, Katie. I am so sorry, sweetie." He pulled Katie from her meditations and into a hug. She would never admit it, but he never begrudged her a shoulder to cry on, whether because of how hard he was working her, or because she needed the support and his was unconditional, so long as she paid for the session with him first. "We just have to find you a new man. Or a temporary playmate."

Katie started laughing, unable to hide her blush from her friend and trainer, emotions settling with the change in topic.

"Who are you hiding from Mario? What's his name? That's the grin of a woman who's just gotten the best sex of her life. Come, come, tell me, or you're going to be doing Crane pose for twenty minutes."

She grinned. "A friend from college offered to console me, and I accepted."

"Girl! Is he hot? Is he married?"

"No, to married. Yes, to hot, very hot."

"That's man material to me, honey. The best way to get over an ex-husband is to get under a new man." He stared at her in his sassy way that she found endearing. "And by the look on your face, the new man was better than the old."

Katie doubled over laughing.

Mario had no idea.

But Doug was no ordinary man. He was a man that was never to be caught.

That didn't mean she wouldn't love to be the woman that changed his mind though.

Chapter 11

"Arthur, I'm so sorry?"

"Will she be ok?"

"Of course I'll be there. You can count on it."

What dumb luck. Her overseas visitors decided to stay over the weekend and she made plans with Doug. Her manager, Arthur was supposed to entertain but his daughter was ill so he wouldn't be there. She had to represent Parker Logistics.

This would have been her second date with Doug. She had to cancel two times already because of her career. Doug would understand. He was an overachiever himself. Who else would put themselves through medical school and law school but an overachiever?

She dialed him up.

"If it isn't the elusive Ms. Katie. Are we still on for this evening or are you cancelling on me?"

Katie sighed. "No, I'm so sorry Doug. I'm dressed and ready to go but my manager called me a few minutes ago. His daughter is sick and I have to make a presentation for him. I know this is last minute. I hope you understand. I'll make it up to you."

"I think I expected that answer," Doug said, the tone of his voice veering on impatience. "You call me when you're available."

"I'll make it up to you. I promise. I've got to go."

"Yeah. We'll talk soon, Katie."

Katie's pulled out her planner to update it for the change of events. She skimmed through it and realized that she has quite a workload. The export position had grown tremendously and she was sinking fast and it was affecting her love life.

She decided to talk to her manager about getting more assistance. She could delegate some of her daily duties so she could focus on the major challenges.

Delegation of duties would ensure her climb up the corporate ladder, but if she was strangled with daily work, she wouldn't get far.

She's had to make time for her life, not just her career.

***

"Melinda, this job is ruining my chances with Doug. I've cancelled three times already. I don't want him to lose interest," Katie exclaimed through the phone.

"Did you call him about the theater tickets?"

"I did but he didn't answer. I think he gave up."

"How long has it been since you talked to him?"

"A few weeks," Katie said disappointedly.

"Give him time. He'll call," Mel said flatly.

As soon as Katie hung up the phone it rang again. She smiled when she recognized Doug's number. "Hello, this is Katie."

"Katie, this is Doug. Are you available to go out Thursday?"

"Let me check my calendar." She reached across the bed to grab it. Flipping the page to Thursday, she let out a moan. "Oh no, I can't. I'm flying to Europe on a business trip. Can we make it sooner?"

"How's Wednesday?"

"That's no good either. I have several things to pack. Well maybe after I come back. I'll call you."

"Thanks Katie, I'll speak to you soon."

After the disappointing phone call with Doug, she called Melinda back so she could complain about her woes.

"Mel speaking"

"You won't believe what happened." Katie said with exasperation. "Doug called to go out on Thursday and I'm leaving the country. Why can't we get together?"

"Why can't you get together?"

"I've got to pack for this business trip and I'll be gone for another three weeks. This was the last chance I had before I leave."

"Don't panic, Katie. And, if nothing else, get some sexy lingerie from Paris. He won't forget you then."

"Mel!" Katie laughed, glad her friend had managed to cheer her up despite her concerns. "I've got to pack."

"You've got to do something about that career" Melinda said emphatically. "I don't work and I make time for everything. I may hop on a flight and we can shop over the weekend. Which country France or UK?"

"Ok. France."

"Did you ask Doug to meet you for a long weekend in Paris? That would be so romantic."

"No," Katie giggled. "He works like I do. I'll have plenty of time when I return."

Chapter 12

Katie arrived at her north side Atlanta home on Thursday and unpacked from her European business trip.

Who would have thought that a three-week trip would cause so much exhaustion? Of course, based off the last business trip she'd taken, it wasn't surprising that her emotions were running high, even though she was walking into an empty house.

She took a hot shower, thinking of her plans for that night if she managed to get Doug on the phone.

Make-up dinner for the last one she'd spoiled…and make-up other events, just for fun.

She smiled as she dialed Doug's cell phone which went to voice mail.

She tried calling his house.

"Bader residence, Lisa speaking."

Who the hell was Lisa?

Katie frowned at the voice on the end of the line.

It was late at night for a housekeeper to answer the phone, but she kept strange hours so she couldn't begrudge Doug his.

"Hi. Is Doug available? This is Katie Pennington."

"No, he isn't. He stepped out with Melissa."

"Oh, no problem. Please don't bother to tell him I called, it was nothing urgent anyways. I'll just try him later."

She didn't wait for a reply, hanging up the phone quickly and staring at the black handset.

Lisa.

Melissa.

How many women did Doug have on his arm?

And where did that leave Katie?

Chapter 13

After a long day at work, Katie stopped by the country club for dinner and drinks to reward herself for putting her life in order. She'd spent the last two weeks on herself: shopping, nails, body waxing, exercising, and getting back into a routine.

Her position was very demanding. Every shipment going overseas had to have the proper paperwork and licenses attached. One false move and a government raid could put her company in jeopardy. She was constantly educating herself on the current laws and common practices as ITAR and EAR.

As dry as it sounded, her job was an exercise for her mind. The challenges the position brought kept her from being bored.

It also kept her from focusing on her ex-disaster of a marriage.

The problem was the job was not considered sexy. Talking to men about her position often was a turn off. Men often fit into two categories: sports and stock market. She didn't have a big interest in sports and followed the stock market as it related to daddy's money, but not much else.

And the man she wanted to see was sitting there, just like he was waiting for her.

Doug, Harold, her attorney, and Greg Speaks, an executive at Parker Logistics, were sitting at a table in the dining room. The men seemed to be having a laugh so she walked over to see if she could join them.

She stepped up behind Doug, let her hand linger on his shoulder before she leaned forward and said her introductions. "Hello gentlemen. What's new?"

Doug's head turned to meet her gaze, his blue eyes alive with merriment.

Harold, spoke first, "Tell Katie your news, Doug."

Doug glanced at the other man then smiled at Katie before breaking his news. "I'm getting married in February."

Katie's mouth fell open. She pulled away from him, a natural reaction to shock but still she couldn't help the near horror that must have crossed her face at his admission. "What? I mean—" She blushed at her response, unable to comprehend how someone else had snagged Doug when she thought *she* was in the running. "Congratulations, Doug."

Trying to keep her smile in place was painful after all she'd been through and all her hopes on this man.

Harold continued, "And—"

And? God, what else could he have to admit?

Doug growled playfully at his friend though the smile on his face didn't dim. "Lisa's expecting."

Lisa?

That was the woman who answered his phone two weeks ago.

She was marrying Doug?

But Katie hadn't been gone that long in Europe!

She'd only missed a couple dates with Doug. Did she mean so little to him?

"That's wonderful." Every word felt like it choked her though she managed to feign interest as best she could over the ache in her heart. "How did you two meet?"

"It's all Greg's fault."

Her coworker leaned back and acted as if stabbed. She hadn't spent a lot of time with Greg at the office, but she'd always heard he was a comedian. Right now his mimed impression wasn't funny to her though she tried to laugh with Harold and Doug at his antics.

"Greg dared me to go over and talk to her," Doug said.

"No, as I recall, I bet you couldn't get her number. I didn't expect you to marry her and get her pregnant." Greg joined in the laughter at the table and Katie stared at them.

She couldn't believe this exchange.

Doug had met a woman on a bet.

He'd met Katie at her divorce, dated her afterwards, and sure, they might have had a few issues with meeting up but that didn't mean he should throw it all away on a floozy he met on a damn bet?

"So when did all this happen?" Katie asked.

Harold motioned for Katie to have a seat.

Doug just smiled and nodded like everything was dandy between them.

She sat down.

She hoped no one noticed that she couldn't quite close her mouth or that the supposed twinkle in her eye was more than likely the beginning of tears.

Doug answered, "About two months ago. We've almost been inseparable since. She would have been here tonight but she had soccer practice and wanted me to spend time with my friends."

Two months?

But she hadn't been gone that long!

They'd had dates and plans and she'd cancelled sure, but he'd called her that last time and that was only a month, at most, ago so how could he have been with Lisa for...

Greg said, "You better enjoy that now because when that baby comes, I won't see you anymore."

He'd been with his fiancée for two months.

"Greg, you're next."

She'd thought he was still with her two months ago.

"Doug, don't throw that jinx my way. Bambi is already itching for me to commit and we've only been dating a month."

But he was uncatchable? He didn't have relationships, only affairs.

"You saw how fast it went for me. Harold and I can't be the only ones bouncing babies. You had better join the group."

She was just another affair for him, a woman to sleep with without the commitment of a relationship.

Which was what she thought she wanted.

But she wanted him.

She still wanted him.

She didn't know what to say.

She still didn't know who the hell Lisa was but it was becoming more and more apparent that the men around her didn't realize what this all meant to her feelings.

Doug especially.

"No way, Doug you sold out on me, and with a sistah at that. The brothers are all going to be mad at you for taking her off the market."

She snorted, and the men laughed around her, not realizing it was self-deprecating, that she was laughing at herself, at the fact that she had the worst choice in men and couldn't turn aside even knowing it.

That she'd lost out to a black woman, and wasn't that just perfect.

"Not as mad as I'm going to be if they don't stay away from my family."

Harold said, "Let's not go there again. We don't need Rocky showing his muscles."

They were all still laughing.

Katie tried to smile but felt the strain of it around her eyes. The men around her looked at her like they'd forgotten she was there. She apologized that she couldn't stay and made as unobtrusive an exit as she could, not that they paid her enough attention to notice.

Doug barely even glanced at her when she rose from her chair, waved away Greg's hand to help her up and walked away.

Doug was too busy thinking about his black fiancée to remember the woman he'd left behind.

Chapter 14

Where had she gone wrong?

She was a sleek, 5'4" blonde. Sea green eyes and a healthy tan from running outside especially during the summer.

She and Doug would have made a good match.

Good families. Career oriented. A full understanding of the struggles of relationships, what with her divorces and his legal practice.

The biggest problem was that Doug had no desire to be a husband...but apparently, she was wrong about that too!

Arriving at her house, she slammed down her briefcase and took her planner and threw it across the room. It landed skidding across her coffee table knocking her crystal coaster onto the floor.

"I can't believe this. Why can't I find someone that I can trust?"

With her best friend Andrea now deleted from her rolodex and her life, she contemplated calling Melinda. They were becoming closer friends, but it wasn't the same as what she'd lost.

But with no one else to call, she punched the numbers into her phone.

"Come on Mel. Answer. I need you."

On the third ring Melinda cheerily answered but her voice quickly turned to concern after hearing the news.

"Are you serious? Doug Bader is getting married to a black woman. If I had known he liked black women I would have told you to start going to the tanning bed just to get some color!"

Katie laughed at her friend's joke, but wasn't relieved. "Melinda, I have no idea what to say. I was in Europe and by the time I got back, I missed my chance with him. I wish I knew what she did to catch him. I didn't think anyone could catch Doug Bader."

"Well, screw him. He's off the market but you're not. You don't need him. Find someone else. Are you going to start internet dating?"

"No, no, I—" Katie hesitated, not sure how to react to everything, not wanting to see another man for a very long time. "No. I have too much work to do and all the men around here are assholes. I'd rather focus on my job than waste time on another idiot."

"Here, here, Katie. You don't need them anyways."

Katie smiled at her friend's support.

"Let's meet for lunch over the weekend. I'll have to tell you about the Botox party I went to. You would love this doctor, Katie. He can take twenty years off your face!"

"You're barely thirty-five Melinda. So, he made you look like a kindergartener again?"

The laughter healed some of the ache in Katie's chest, but she still went to sleep thinking of Doug and the ring she wouldn't wear on her finger.

Bastard.

Chapter 15

Katie prepared for the silent auction at Dupree Country Club. She was wearing a full-length shimmering blue gown, black heels, blue matching purse, sparkling diamond earrings and her hair was swept up in a sexy cascading bun. Her choices were very slim for the type of man she needed on her arm for this event.

So her dad was her man of the hour.

Don arrived in a stretch limousine. Katie walked to the car with her head held high and waited for the chauffer to open the door for her. Her dad was already seated and waiting. The ride was very silent as Katie was still replaying the marriage over in her head and the betrayal of her best friend and her husband.

"Look Katie, I know it looks glum, and it's been very tough since your mom passed away. I've tried to be the one you can come to for all your problems. I know your mom would be here giving you her support, but sometimes it just takes a couple tries before you meet the right person."

Don's words pulled Katie out of her thoughts.

"Is that why you're still hitting on everything with some curves and two legs, Dad? How many tries before you find the right one? Are you really trying?"

"I'm a tired old cynic, princess. You're too young to be like me."

The floodgate of tears started and she couldn't hold them back. Just once couldn't everything just go right in her life?

Don offered his hanky and Katie started dabbing the tears one at a time until too many came. She leaned on his shoulder and he embraced her as the tears flowed into his tie and started to soak a baseball size watermark on his Armani shirt.

Katie's wails grew louder as she held her dad tight.

Don sat silent to allow his daughter to release the grief that she so bravely held in.

"I'm so sorry, Dad," she sputtered in between sobs. "I couldn't help it."

"I know. Dry your tears. It will get better. I promise. Even if I have to pay for it."

Katie sniffled as she finished drying her tears.

She fished through the bottom of her purse to grab her dark sunglasses and put them on her puffy face.

After all, she was a Pennington.

Brave, strong, and above all pressures.

She could survive anything, and she didn't need anyone else to do it with.

The limo pulled to a stop in front of the club.

"I'm ready. Let's go in."

***

Everyone at the place was dressed in formal attire. Many of the men were in black tuxedos some breaking the tradition and wearing white.

Through the crowd of people, she saw Doug. That sandy blonde hair was unmistakable. He was with a black female, shoulder length hair, gold dress, black heels, and black purse. That must be Lisa. Her hand was locked in Doug's.

Katie wanted a closer look. Doug was talking to Harold and a woman who appeared to be his wife. She was holding his hand loosely, looking very pregnant and wearing a white loose gown that was appropriate for her condition. Is everyone in life pregnant?

Katie approached the couples.

"Doug, how are you this evening? You look good in a tux." She extended her hand to Lisa in introduction. She cut her eyes low and high to size up her *supposed* competition. "I'm Katie Pennington, and you are?"

Lisa sucked in a breath but before she could respond, Katie turned to Harold. "So good to see you, Harold. Is this your wife?"

"And you, Katie. And yes, this is my wife, Hannah," Harold said proudly. "We were just talking about babies and everything. We're expecting our first in April."

"Congratulations" Katie said in a falsetto voice that was almost good enough for a Broadway musical. She turned to further observe Doug and Lisa.

Lisa was smiling from ear to ear, blushing softly, clutching Doug's hand proudly displaying her gold ring on freshly colored peach fingernails.

Doug's eyes sparkled through his dark rimmed glasses. He pulled Lisa closer to him.

That should have been Katie.

He met Katie's gaze. "This is my fiancée, Lisa."

Katie straightened her back and shifted her stance, her perfect red bottomed Louboutins shoulder width apart like she was readying for battle.

"Nice to meet you, Kate," Lisa said, extending her hand and waiting for Katie to reach for it.

Probably so she could pull away like Katie had.

She extended her hand, like the formality at the start of competition.

Lisa appeared to be winning.

Not for long.

Katie was a Pennington.

She would be polite.

She would not make a scene.

But she would damn sure win.

"It's Katie." She tried a smile and turned back to Doug, doing her best to ignore the other woman. "How are the plans for the wedding coming?"

Composed. She thought to herself. *I behaved really well.*

She watched as Lisa pulled Doug towards her, gave him a kiss on the cheek.

Deep breaths.

She beat you to him.

But it was not over. Yet.

Doug replied, "They're coming along fine. Lisa's mom and sister are doing a lot of the planning."

Harold and his wife, Hannah, excused themselves from the group leaving the awkward threesome behind.

Katie fought not to sneer at the way Lisa preened, smiling for all she was worth, like the news she was hearing wasn't a load of bullshit to ensnare a wealthy bachelor.

That's what this was. All a ploy to get a "baby daddy" or whatever the phrase was.

The thought made her grit her teeth more. "How nice of them. Have you set a date?"

Katie had to be there.

She couldn't see Doug going through with it. After all, they were in the South. He had a reputation to protect. He was asking for a lot of grief marrying a black girl.

He'd change his mind and leave the bitch standing at the altar.

Doug answered, "Here, first day of February. Lisa wants to keep it simple and she has a lot of soccer players from the girls she coaches who want to attend so we need a large venue. Are you coming?"

Lisa looked at Doug as if he'd lost his mind.

Katie noticed the tension and made a devilish grin. "My invitation must be lost in the mail."

"We have some extras at home."

Katie watched Lisa's alarm turn to a fake smile.

"Of course you're invited. The wedding is at 4:30 with the reception to follow."

"Great. Wouldn't miss it. I'll make sure to mark it on my calendar." Katie smiled at Lisa, hoping it came off as warm even as she hoped the marriage failed. "Congratulations to the both of you."

"Thank you," Doug replied.

Lisa tugged on his arm. "Doug, I think I need to sit. I feel a little dizzy."

Doug and Lisa excused themselves from Katie and Katie watched them walk away, the ever-attentive bachelor catering to his black fiancée's every whim.

"We'll see how long that lasts," Katie thought, deciding that she'd had enough for the night and didn't actually want to watch the two *love birds* make kissy faces.

Besides, it would be more fun to prepare for the wedding to come.

She'd be there to pick Doug up when he walked away from the other woman.

Katie ignored the hint of sympathy at the idea of being left behind, and forced herself to focus on getting what she wanted.

After all, someone had to fulfill all her needs, why shouldn't it be herself taking care of business?

For the next instalment in the Southern Men Don't Fall in Love series, visit:

www.MiaMaeLynne.com

ABOUT THE AUTHOR

MIA MAE LYNNE - has enjoyed writing from the time she was in grade school. She started a diary and wrote in the journal for seven years. She always knew that one day all her creative ideas would come into fruition and writing has been her escape.

"The Chronicles of Fate" series was born in the metro Atlanta area allowing her to explore her creative side. The series was later renamed to "Southern Men Don't Fall in Love" with "Atlanta's Most Eligible Bachelor" as the first book in the series with many more to follow. She has enjoyed writing the series and has embraced each of the characters as they have entrusted her with their stories to share with the world.

After discovering psychic and mediumship abilities, she became a student of spiritualism. She has newly begun this path and has explored the traditional areas of tarot, numerology, astrology and other related areas of interest in the metaphysical arts. She has received training from the Fellowship of the Spirit in New York as well as read numerous books and attended various classes to expand her knowledge.

www.ingramcontent.com/pod-product-compliance
Lightning Source LLC
Chambersburg PA
CBHW020636130626
46552CB00003B/1261